D1572869

May your life be full of great adventures- be <u>brave!</u>

Best Wishes,

Ben

Bryson the Brave

Written by Ben Aubee

Illustrated by Pinkoei

Bryson the Brave/written by Ben Aubee, 1st ed.

ISBN: 978-0-578-87605-4

To my son, Bryson - may you always be kind and brave.
I love you more than the rabbit loves his new tail.

Bryson was a bison who wasn't very tall.

Compared to the others, he was really quite small.

Bryson was different than the others.

Some would say there was something wrong with his colors.

Bryson's fur was white like the moon,

It stuck out when the herd would commune.

Springtime arrived and North the herd headed.

Snow melted, flowers bloomed, winter had finally ended!

Bryson and the other calves would all hang out.

They'd romp around and play and shout.

One of the calves was huge and wooly.

He wasn't very nice and was actually kind of a bully.

Thunder was the bully's name,

Pushing around the others was his favorite game.

One day, two magpies flew down from the sky.

"We're so tired," they cried, "can we steal a ride?"

"Get lost you silly birds," Thunder replied.

But Bryson just winked, happy to give any help he could provide.

After the birds were well-rested, they flew off with a cry, "Goodbye!"

Bryson just nodded and smiled in reply.

One bird said to the other – "That Bryson is so kind.

He'll always be a friend of mine."

The next morning, Bryson saw Thunder stomping around.

He looked closer and saw a mouse on the ground.

Bryson charged into Thunder, to his dismay,

Giving the mouse just enough time to get away.

Thunder bellowed, "Stay out of my way!"

He knocked Bryson down and shouted, "Next time you'll pay!"

The mouse looked out from under a bush nearby,

She said, "Bryson saved my life," with a tear in her eye.

Later that day, as the sun started to set,

A young pronghorn ran by as fast as a jet.

He shouted to the calves, "Come play with me.

I'm the fastest here, you'll see!"

Thunder sneered, "Ha, me play with you? No."

But Bryson smiled and said, "Let's go!"

The two played for a while, wild and free.

They were both pretty fast, they agreed.

The herd was homeward bound upon the trail,

When Bryson heard the crying of a cottontail.

He found the rabbit and asked if he was okay.

The rabbit sobbed, "I lost my tail in a fire the other day!"

Bryson thought for a moment - "I have an idea," he said.

Then he lay down and wallowed until he started to shed.

"I don't need all this fur anymore,

But it looks like there's something you can use it for!"

He rolled a piece into a small ball for the bunny,

who stuck it to his rump and said, "Now isn't that funny!

I have a tail again it seems!

In fact, it's so thick and fluffy, it's the tail of my dreams!"

Later that night, the herd was settling down,
when the calves heard a slight rustling sound.
Out of the bushes crawled a little gray fox,
"Can I snuggle up with you til the rain stops?"

Thunder snarled, "Scram Fox Pup!"

But Bryson whispered, "Come on over and cuddle up!"

Despite the cold rain, Bryson and the fox were quite cozy.

They awoke the next morning and their outlooks were rosy.

The little fox went on her way and said, "Goodbye my friend, I really hope to see you again!"

A few days later, the bison were almost home.

Thunder said to the other calves, "Come on, let's go roam!"

One of the calves looked to the woods - "We shouldn't go there,

My mom told me there could be bears!"

Thunder ran off ahead.

"Come on you sissies," he said.

He galloped around a corner and the others heard him yelp.

"Guys, there's a grizzly bear! Come quick, I need help!"

The other calves turned around and ran.

But Bryson thought, "I need to help Thunder if I can!"

He hollered and ran towards the bear,

But the grizzly only turned with a glare.

Bryson said, "Hey, leave my friend alone!"

But the bear's anger had only grown.

The bear began to scowl,

And started towards Bryson with a fierce growl.

Suddenly, the bear halted in his tracks.

He changed his mind and stopped his attack.

Bryson turned around confused,

He saw what was behind him and was quite amused.

All the animals he met on his trip,

Stood with their friends, hip-to-hip.

The bear turned around and ran away,

Bryson hugged his friends as they all yelled, "Hooray!"

They said, "Bryson, you're so kind and brave!"

"We've met many bison, but you'll always be our fave!"

It was time to rejoin the others,

So they headed back to their bison sisters and brothers.

Thunder and Bryson trotted back to the herd,

As Thunder muttered, "you better not tell them I was saved by birds."

THE END

About the Author

Ben Aubee lives in Middletown, RI with his wife, Ashley, and son, Bryson. He is a healthcare IT consultant, loves traveling and music, and co-owns Rejects Beer Company, also in Middletown, RI. His motivation for writing "Bryson the Brave" came from his son's love of reading and he hopes this journey will help inspire Bryson to be brave and never stop trying new things. The editing assistance of his beautiful wife along with the values instilled in him by his parents, Tom and Paula Aubee, helped him craft this tale. He hopes it's enjoyed by all those who read it.

About the Illustrator

Pinkoei is a young artist based in Sao Bento do Sul, Brazil. Since childhood, he dreamt of creating his own illustrations for others to enjoy. Now he is a professional illustrator.

CPSIA information can be obtained
at www.ICGtesting.com
Printed in the USA
BVHW060041030821
612776BV00001B/5